A Smile of Betrayal- A Novel

Sagor sarker

Published by Sagor Sarker, 2024.

A SMILE OF BETRAYAL- A NOVEL

First edition. November 21, 2024.

ISBN: 979-8227166036

Written by Sagor sarker.

Also by Sagor sarker

The Poetry of Lover's Heart
The Rise of Darkness
Love in Quiet Tremors
The Last Breath of a Love
Embrace Of Sweet Tomorrows
A Smile of Betrayal- A Novel

Watch for more at https://www.facebook.com/sagor.sarker.334/.

A Smile of Betrayal- A Novel

A Smile of Betrayal is a fast-paced thriller about trust, betrayal, and the dark secrets people keep. The story follows Jordan, a strong-willed protagonist who sets out to uncover a traitor in their midst. What begins as a mission to expose a hidden enemy soon turns into a deadly game of lies and manipulation, where no one can be trusted.

As Jordan and their allies dive deeper into a world of deception, they discover that the traitor they've been hunting is much closer than they thought. With twists at every corner, the lines between friend and foe begin to blur, and Jordan must confront shocking truths that will change everything they thought they knew.

In the end, it's not just about survival—it's about breaking free from a dangerous web of power and control. A Smile of Betrayal is packed with suspense, unexpected turns, and a cast of characters who will keep you guessing until the very end.

If you enjoy gripping stories filled with intrigue, betrayal, and a fight for freedom, this novel is for you.

By- Sagor sarker

A Smile of Betrayal- A Novel

Chapter 1: The First Visitor

It was raining outside. Not the angry, thunder-filled rain, but a slow, rhythmic drizzle that soaked the city quietly, as if trying to cleanse it. Jordan Cross sat by the window of their small, cluttered office, a mug of untouched coffee in hand, staring blankly at the drops sliding down the glass. There was something comforting about this kind of rain—it filled the silence but didn't demand attention.

The knock on the door was soft. Hesitant. Jordan glanced at the clock: 7:14 PM. Clients didn't usually show up unannounced this late. With a sigh, they set the mug down and walked to the door.

The woman standing on the other side was not what Jordan expected. She looked like she belonged in one of those old black-and-white photographs—graceful, poised, and distant. Her silver-gray hair was perfectly styled, her black coat spotless despite the rain. The only thing out of place was her eyes. They were sharp, restless, and searching.

"Jordan Cross?" she asked, her voice clipped and precise.

Jordan nodded, stepping aside to let her in. The woman walked in, surveying the room like she was assessing a crime scene. She didn't sit until Jordan gestured to the worn leather chair across the desk.

"Eleanor Vale," she introduced herself. "I believe you've heard of my family."

Jordan had. The Vales were one of those wealthy, untouchable families that tabloids loved to write about. Old money. Big scandals. They hadn't been in the news for a while, but the name was familiar enough.

"I need your help," Eleanor said, cutting straight to the point. "My daughter-in-law, Alice, has been missing for six months."

Jordan leaned back in their chair, folding their arms. "And you don't trust the police?"

Eleanor's lips tightened. "The police are incompetent. They've found nothing. But Alice didn't just vanish. Someone in my family knows what happened to her."

Jordan raised an eyebrow. "And you think they'll tell me?"

"I don't expect them to. That's why I need you. You don't just find the truth. You make people reveal it." She placed an envelope on the desk. It was thick, stuffed with cash. "I don't care what it costs."

Jordan stared at the envelope but didn't reach for it. "Why now?" they asked. "Why come to me after six months?"

Eleanor hesitated, her mask of confidence slipping for just a moment. "Because I received this yesterday." She pulled out a photograph from her coat pocket and slid it across the desk.

Jordan picked it up. The image was grainy, but there was no mistaking the figure in the foreground. It was Alice Vale, sitting in what looked like a café, her face turned away from the camera. The timestamp in the corner was from two weeks ago.

"That's impossible," Eleanor said quietly. "Alice is dead. I know she is."

Jordan studied the photograph, their mind already racing. "What do you want me to do?"

"Find out where she is," Eleanor said, her voice hardening again. "Find out who's lying."

Outside, the rain continued to fall, each drop tapping against the window like a question Jordan wasn't sure they wanted to answer.

Chapter 2: Threads of Deceit

The rain hadn't let up, but Jordan barely noticed it as they stood by the window, the photograph still in hand. Alice Vale. Missing, presumed dead—or so the world believed. Yet here she was, frozen in time, alive just two weeks ago. Jordan couldn't decide what felt heavier: the weight of the photograph or the questions it carried.

Behind them, Eleanor Vale sat perfectly still, her eyes fixed on Jordan like a predator watching prey.

"This is all you have?" Jordan asked, turning to face her.

"For now."

Jordan placed the photograph on the desk. "For someone who doesn't trust the police, you seem awfully certain Alice is dead. Care to explain?"

Eleanor's jaw tightened, her gloved hands resting delicately on her lap. "Intuition," she said after a pause, her tone clipped. "When you've lived as long as I have, you learn to trust it."

Jordan smirked. "Intuition doesn't hold up in court, Mrs. Vale. If you want my help, you'll need to be honest with me. All of it."

Eleanor's gaze didn't waver, but a flicker of something—hesitation, annoyance—crossed her face. "Very well," she said at last. "Alice was... complicated. She had a talent for making enemies. My family, myself included, never quite trusted her. She had this... charm, a way of making you feel as though you were the only person in the room. It made her dangerous."

"Dangerous how?"

"She wasn't a Vale," Eleanor said simply, as though that explained everything. "She married into us. That may not mean much to you, but in our world, it matters. And Alice knew it. She played her role beautifully, but she always had her own agenda. I could feel it."

Jordan leaned forward, folding their hands. "And what exactly was this 'agenda'?"

Eleanor's lips pressed into a thin line. For a moment, Jordan thought she wouldn't answer. Then, quietly: "She wanted control. Over my son. Over this family. I don't know how far she was willing to go, but if Alice is still alive, she's dangerous. You need to understand that."

Jordan nodded slowly, filing the words away. "And what about the rest of your family? How do they feel about Alice?"

Eleanor's expression shifted, her gaze turning distant. "Graham adored her, of course. He's my son; he sees what he wants to see. But my daughter, Lila... well, let's just say Lila has always been protective of what's hers."

"And Victor?" Jordan asked.

Eleanor's composure cracked, just slightly. "Victor? What does he have to do with this?"

"I don't know yet. But I like to be thorough."

Eleanor rose from her seat, smoothing her coat with precise movements. "Victor is irrelevant. Focus on Alice. And the clock is ticking, Mr. Cross."

"It's *Jordan*," they corrected, but Eleanor was already heading for the door.

Before leaving, she paused, her hand on the doorknob. "I'll expect updates. Daily."

The door closed softly behind her, leaving Jordan alone with the photograph and a growing sense of unease.

Later That Night

The office was dark except for the dim glow of the desk lamp. Jordan sat with their laptop open, pulling up files on the Vale family. It didn't take long to confirm what they already knew: the Vales were old money, steeped in power and scandal. Graham Vale, the grieving husband, was the head of a prominent investment firm. Lila Vale, his sister, had a reputation for being the wild one—a socialite with a knack for trouble. And Victor Vale...

Jordan frowned at the screen. Victor Vale was harder to pin down. No official job title, no public appearances, no social media presence. Yet his name popped up in connection with a few unsavory dealings: offshore accounts, anonymous donations to questionable charities. He was the kind of man who thrived in shadows.

But it wasn't just Victor's file that bothered Jordan. It was the nagging feeling that they'd met him before. Somewhere, years ago, in a past life they'd rather forget.

The photograph lay on the desk beside the laptop. Jordan picked it up again, studying Alice's face. There was something about her expression—calm, almost amused. As if she knew she was being watched and didn't care.

Jordan's phone buzzed, pulling them out of their thoughts. The number was unlisted.

"Cross," they answered.

A voice crackled on the other end. "You shouldn't have taken the case."

Jordan sat up straight. "Who is this?"

Silence. Then, a low chuckle. "Some truths aren't meant to be uncovered."

The line went dead.

Jordan stared at the phone, the unease from earlier now a full-blown storm. Outside, the rain had finally stopped, leaving the city eerily quiet.

Somewhere out there, Alice Vale was alive—or someone wanted them to believe she was. Either way, Jordan knew one thing for certain: this wasn't just about a missing woman. It was about power, control, and secrets someone was willing to kill for.

And they were right in the middle of it.

Chapter 3: The Vale Mansion

The Vale mansion wasn't what Jordan expected.

Driving up the long, gravel-lined path, they had pictured something ostentatious—white pillars, sprawling fountains, the kind of wealth that flaunted itself shamelessly. Instead, the house rose like a dark monolith against the overcast sky, its slate-gray stone weathered by time. Ivy crept along its walls, and the windows, though large, seemed to peer out like eyes, watching Jordan's car approach.

A guard at the gate had waved them through without a word, as if they were expected. By the time Jordan reached the wide front steps, they were already drenched in an uneasy feeling that had nothing to do with the lingering mist in the air.

The heavy oak door creaked open before Jordan could knock. A young woman, no older than twenty, stood there, her uniform crisp and her expression neutral.

"You must be Mr. Cross," she said, her tone so polite it felt rehearsed. "Please, come in."

"It's *Jordan*," they corrected automatically, but the woman didn't respond. She turned on her heel, leading them into a cavernous foyer.

The interior was grand, yes, but in a way that felt frozen in time. The polished floors gleamed, and a massive crystal chandelier hung above, but the air smelled faintly of old wood and something metallic. Portraits of solemn-faced ancestors lined the walls, their painted eyes following Jordan as they moved.

"Mrs. Vale is in the sitting room," the maid said, gesturing toward a door on the left before disappearing down the hall.

Jordan hesitated, taking in the room. There was something about this place—its silence, its stillness—that felt wrong, as if the house itself were holding its breath. Shaking off the thought, they pushed open the door.

The Sitting Room

Eleanor Vale was waiting, as composed as ever. She sat by the fireplace, a porcelain teacup balanced delicately in her hand.

"You're early," she remarked, though her tone suggested she wasn't surprised.

"I like to get a sense of my surroundings," Jordan replied, stepping inside.

The room was warm, filled with the crackling sound of the fire, but it did little to soften Eleanor's presence. She gestured to a chair across from her, and Jordan sat, noticing the small table between them. On it lay a file folder, thick and well-used.

"You'll want to review this," Eleanor said, pushing it toward them.

Jordan opened it, their eyes skimming over the contents: photographs of Alice, notes from the police investigation, a timeline of her last known movements. At the bottom of the stack was a letter, handwritten and smeared in places.

"What's this?" Jordan asked, holding it up.

"Alice's handwriting," Eleanor replied. "We found it in her room a week after she disappeared. It's... cryptic, but perhaps it means something to you."

Jordan scanned the letter. The words were fragmented, almost poetic:

They're watching.

Every move, every word.

I am a thread in their tapestry, and I must unravel before they do.

Jordan frowned. "This doesn't read like someone planning to run. It sounds more like paranoia."

Eleanor's lips thinned. "Alice had her demons."

"Such as?"

Before Eleanor could respond, the door opened abruptly, and a man entered. His presence filled the room, tall and broad-shouldered, with dark hair that fell in neat waves. His face was handsome but drawn, like someone who hadn't slept in weeks.

"Graham," Eleanor said smoothly. "I wasn't expecting you."

Jordan rose, extending a hand. "Jordan Cross."

Graham ignored it, his eyes narrowing as he looked them over. "The interrogator."

Jordan let their hand drop, unfazed. "Your mother hired me to look into Alice's disappearance."

"Did she also tell you to dig through our private lives?" Graham's tone was sharp, his anger barely contained.

"Graham," Eleanor said, her voice a warning.

"No, Mother, let's not pretend this is normal," he snapped. "Bringing a stranger into our home to dig up dirt? What are you hoping to find?"

"The truth," Jordan said calmly, meeting his glare. "That's why I'm here. Unless there's something you don't want me to uncover."

Graham's jaw tightened, but he said nothing. Instead, he turned on his heel and left the room, the door slamming shut behind him.

Eleanor sighed, setting down her teacup. "I apologize for my son. This has been... difficult for him."

"Difficult for all of you, I'm sure," Jordan said, though their mind was already racing. Graham's anger wasn't surprising, but it felt per formative. Like a show meant to distract.

Exploring the Mansion

After the meeting, Eleanor allowed Jordan free rein of the house. They wandered through its halls, each room a snapshot of the Vale family's past. The library smelled of leather and dust, its shelves lined with books that looked more decorative than read. A locked study caught Jordan's attention, but a maid appeared before they could inspect it further.

Eventually, Jordan found themselves in the gallery, a long corridor filled with portraits and photographs. At the far end, a single photograph stood out. It was newer than the others, its frame sleek and modern.

It was Alice, her smile radiant, standing beside Graham. Her hand rested on his arm, but her eyes... her eyes were elsewhere.

Jordan leaned closer, noting the faint reflection of another figure in the background, blurred but unmistakable. It was Victor Vale.

A chill ran down their spine.

This wasn't just a family with secrets. This was a family with shadows—and Alice, it seemed, had been trying to escape them all.

Chapter 4: Shadows in the Dark

Jordan hadn't planned to meet Victor Vale that night.

The gallery's unnerving silence followed them as they turned back toward the main hall. But as they reached the top of the grand staircase, a low voice echoed behind them.

"Admiring the family?"

Jordan spun around. Standing in the shadows at the end of the corridor was a man with a lean frame and an aura that demanded attention. He stepped into the dim light, revealing sharp features and a faint smirk that didn't quite reach his eyes.

Victor Vale.

Unlike Eleanor or Graham, Victor had an air of disinterest, as though the mansion, the family, and even Jordan were little more than minor inconveniences.

"You're Victor," Jordan said, keeping their tone neutral.

"And you're the interrogator," Victor replied, his voice smooth but laced with something unreadable. "The one digging into our lives."

"Just doing my job," Jordan said, crossing their arms.

Victor chuckled softly, stepping closer. "Your job. Right. And what exactly do you think you'll find here? A missing woman? A guilty conscience? Or are you just here to justify that fat check my dear sister-in-law paid you?"

Jordan didn't flinch, but the insinuation stung. "I'm here to find the truth. Unless you have something to hide?"

Victor tilted his head, his smile widening. "The truth," he repeated, as though tasting the word. "Do you know what's funny about the truth, Mr. Cross? It's never as clean as people like you think it is. It's messy. Ugly. And sometimes, it's better left buried."

Jordan felt a flicker of unease. Victor's words were deliberate, like a predator circling prey.

"Speaking from experience?" Jordan asked, refusing to back down.

Victor's smile faltered, his eyes narrowing. For a moment, something flickered across his face—recognition, perhaps, or something deeper.

"Let me give you some advice," Victor said, his voice dropping. "This family has a way of consuming people who get too close. You'd be wise to tread carefully."

Before Jordan could respond, Victor turned on his heel and disappeared down the corridor, his footsteps fading into the distance.

Jordan exhaled, their shoulders stiff. They'd dealt with difficult people before, but Victor was different. There was a weight to his words, a quiet menace that felt personal.

The Study

Jordan couldn't shake the encounter as they wandered back through the house. Something about Victor's warning gnawed at them, and they found themselves drawn to the locked study they had noticed earlier.

The door was still closed, but this time, the hall was empty. After a quick glance to ensure no one was watching, Jordan reached for the small leather pouch they kept in their jacket. A few practiced movements later, the lock clicked open.

Inside, the room was dimly lit by a single desk lamp. Papers were scattered across the desk, along with a half-empty glass of amber liquid. Jordan moved closer, scanning the surface. Most of the papers were financial documents, boring at first glance, until something caught their eye: a list of names.

Alice Vale's name was circled.

Beside it were two others: *Lila Vale* and *Victor Vale.*

Before Jordan could examine it further, a faint noise broke the silence—a shuffle, like someone shifting their weight.

They turned sharply, their eyes darting to the shadows near the door.

"Should I be impressed, or concerned?" a voice drawled.

Victor stood in the doorway, leaning casually against the frame. He held a cigarette between his fingers, the faint ember glowing in the darkness.

Jordan cursed under their breath.

"Breaking and entering," Victor said, taking a slow drag. "Not exactly the mark of a professional."

Jordan stepped back from the desk but didn't bother denying it. "Why don't you tell me why Alice's name is on this list?"

Victor's expression didn't change, but there was a flicker of something in his eyes. He stepped into the room, closing the door behind him.

"That list," he said, his tone light, "isn't your concern."

"It became my concern when your sister-in-law hired me," Jordan shot back.

Victor smirked, leaning against the desk. "You think Eleanor wants the truth? That she's some noble matriarch desperate to find her missing daughter-in-law?"

Jordan said nothing, waiting.

Victor leaned closer. "Let me save you some time, Mr. Cross. Eleanor doesn't want the truth. She wants control. And Alice..." He paused, as if savoring the words. "...was a threat she couldn't afford to keep."

Jordan's stomach twisted. "You think Eleanor had something to do with Alice's disappearance?"

Victor shrugged. "Think what you like. But if I were you, I'd be asking why Eleanor didn't give you that list herself. And I'd start looking at Lila."

Before Jordan could respond, Victor stepped back, his smirk returning. "Consider this a favor. But don't expect another."

With that, he was gone, leaving Jordan alone in the study, their mind racing.

Jordan's Apartment, Later

The rain had returned, drumming softly against the windows of Jordan's apartment. They sat at their desk, the list spread out in front of them. Lila's name stood out now, alongside Alice's and Victor's.

Was Victor trying to misdirect them? Or was he genuinely trying to help? And what role did Eleanor really play in all this?

As Jordan mulled over the possibilities, their phone buzzed. This time, it wasn't an unlisted number. It was Lila Vale.

"Mr. Cross," her voice purred through the line. "I think it's time we talked. Privately."

Jordan's grip tightened on the phone. "What about?"

"I know what happened to Alice," Lila said. "But if you want the truth, you'll have to meet me."

The line went dead before Jordan could reply, leaving them with more questions than answers.

Chapter 5: Secrets by Candlelight

The café Lila Vale had chosen was a sharp contrast to the imposing grandeur of her family's mansion. Tucked away in a quiet corner of the city, it was intimate and dimly lit, its walls adorned with abstract paintings that seemed to twist and shift under the flickering candlelight.

Jordan arrived early, staking out a corner table where they could watch the entrance. Lila swept in fifteen minutes late, wearing a long trench coat and oversized sunglasses, though the evening was far too dark for them. She moved with the confident grace of someone who expected the world to bend to her whims.

"You came," she said, sliding into the seat opposite Jordan and removing her glasses. Her smile was sharp, more predator than pleasantry.

"You didn't leave much of a choice," Jordan replied.

Lila signaled to the waiter for a drink before leaning in, her elbows resting lightly on the table. "Let's skip the small talk, shall we? You're here because you want answers. And I'm here because I'm tired of pretending everything's fine."

Jordan raised an eyebrow. "You make it sound like you've been carrying some heavy secret."

Lila chuckled, low and bitter. "Oh, you have no idea. But let's start with the obvious, shall we? You want to know about Alice."

"That is why I'm here."

Lila's eyes glittered with something unreadable—contempt, regret, maybe both. "Alice was trouble from the moment she entered our lives. Beautiful, clever, manipulative. She knew exactly how to get what she wanted. My brother fell for her hard, of course. Graham's always been the romantic type. But Alice... she had no intention of being the dutiful wife. She was playing a long game."

"What kind of game?" Jordan asked, leaning forward.

Lila hesitated, glancing around the café as if the walls had ears. "Do you know what happens to someone who doesn't fit into a family like ours? Someone who doesn't follow the rules?"

"They get pushed out?"

"They get destroyed," Lila said flatly. "Alice wasn't the victim everyone wants to believe she was. She was dangerous. A master manipulator. And when she finally crossed the line, we had no choice but to—"

She stopped herself, biting her lip.

"No choice but to what?" Jordan pressed.

Lila shook her head, a bitter laugh escaping her lips. "You think you're ready for the truth? You're not. But I'll give you a hint: Alice knew something. Something big enough to tear this family apart. And she wasn't afraid to use it."

Jordan's pulse quickened. "What kind of secret?"

Lila leaned back, her expression turning cold. "If you really want to know, look into Victor. He's the one pulling the strings in this family, not my mother. He always has been."

"Victor says I should be looking at you," Jordan said, watching her closely.

Lila's smile turned icy. "Of course he does. Victor's always been good at deflecting attention. But trust me, he's the one with blood on his hands."

Jordan's mind raced. Lila's words were cryptic, but there was no denying the venom in her tone when she spoke about Victor.

The Warning

As their conversation wound down, Lila reached for her purse, pulling out a small envelope. She slid it across the table to Jordan.

"What's this?" Jordan asked.

"Something Alice left behind," Lila said, her voice quieter now. "I found it after she disappeared, hidden in her room. I don't know what it means, but it's the kind of thing that gets people killed."

Jordan hesitated before taking the envelope. Inside was a single photograph, grainy and slightly out of focus. It showed Alice standing near a car, her back to the camera. In the foreground, a man stood watching her—Victor.

On the back of the photograph, a single word was scrawled in Alice's handwriting: *Leverage.*

"What does this mean?" Jordan asked, holding up the photograph.

"I told you, I don't know," Lila said, rising from her seat. "But whatever Alice was planning, she wasn't afraid of Victor. And that should terrify you."

With that, she slipped on her sunglasses and disappeared into the night, leaving Jordan with more questions than answers.

Back at the Apartment

The photograph sat on Jordan's desk, its presence unsettling. They stared at the word scrawled on the back: *Leverage.*

It was clear now that Alice had been playing a dangerous game, one that involved secrets, power, and betrayal. But who had the most to gain—or lose—from her disappearance?

Jordan's phone buzzed, breaking the silence. It was an unlisted number again.

Against their better judgment, they answered.

"I warned you," came Victor's voice, low and menacing. "But you don't listen, do you?"

"What do you want, Victor?" Jordan demanded.

"To remind you," Victor said, his tone chilling, "that some secrets are worth dying for. And you're getting too close."

The line went dead, leaving Jordan alone with the photograph and the weight of Victor's threat.

Chapter 6: Shadows in the Mirror

Victor's threat lingered in Jordan's mind like a storm cloud, dark and oppressive. But threats, no matter how chilling, weren't enough to deter them. If anything, they fueled Jordan's resolve.

Seated at their desk, they studied the photograph again. The image was ordinary on the surface—a blurry, candid moment—but the context made it dangerous. Alice, standing beside a car. Victor, in the foreground, his posture stiff, his gaze unyielding.

And the word on the back: *Leverage.*

What kind of leverage? Jordan knew the answer wouldn't come from speculation—it would come from action.

The Trail Leads to Victor

Victor was too careful to leave obvious clues, but Jordan had learned long ago that no one was flawless. Everyone made mistakes; it was just a matter of finding them.

Pulling out their laptop, Jordan started digging. They bypassed the Vale family's public-facing reputation—philanthropic endeavors, real estate investments, political connections—and focused on the shadows where power often hid.

It didn't take long to find whispers.

Victor Vale wasn't just a businessman. He had ties to a series of shell companies, many of which had been flagged for suspicious activity: offshore accounts, sudden liquidations, missing assets.

One name stood out in the maze of corporate entities: *Argent Capital.* The company had been dissolved years ago, but before that, it had been embroiled in a lawsuit over embezzlement. The case had been dismissed, but not before drawing attention to an unusual connection: Alice Vale had worked as a consultant for Argent Capital just months before it collapsed.

Jordan's pulse quickened. This wasn't a coincidence.

Before they could dig further, their phone buzzed. A text, this time from an unknown number.

If you want answers, come to the old pier. Midnight. Alone.

Jordan's stomach twisted. The timing was too perfect to ignore.

The Pier

The old pier was a relic of the city's industrial past, its wooden planks rotting and its metal railings rusted from years of neglect. The air was thick with the smell of salt and decay, and the distant hum of the waves created an eerie backdrop.

Jordan parked their car a block away and approached cautiously, their flashlight cutting through the darkness.

"Glad you made it."

The voice came from the shadows, smooth and familiar. Victor stepped into the dim light, his hands tucked into the pockets of his coat.

"You're really going for the whole movie villain aesthetic, huh?" Jordan said, keeping their tone steady.

Victor chuckled softly. "I've been called worse."

"What do you want, Victor?"

"I want to help you," Victor said, his smirk widening.

Jordan didn't buy it for a second. "Help me? By threatening me over the phone?"

"That wasn't a threat," Victor said smoothly. "It was a warning. You're digging into things you don't understand, and you're too smart not to see where this is headed."

Jordan folded their arms. "Then spell it out for me."

Victor sighed, as though indulging a stubborn child. "Fine. You've already figured out that Alice wasn't some innocent victim. She was ambitious, ruthless even. She came into this family with a plan, and she almost succeeded."

"Succeeded at what?" Jordan pressed.

Victor's expression darkened. "Taking everything. The Vale name, the Vale fortune—control. She was smarter than all of us, and she knew it. But she made one mistake."

"What mistake?"

"She underestimated me," Victor said, his voice a low growl. "I knew what she was doing, and I stopped her."

The weight of his words hung in the air, thick and suffocating.

"So you're admitting you had something to do with her disappearance?" Jordan asked.

Victor's smirk returned, but it was colder now. "I'm admitting that Alice played a dangerous game. And when you play with fire, you get burned."

The Unexpected Twist

Before Jordan could respond, the sound of footsteps echoed from the far end of the pier. Both of them turned, their gazes narrowing on the figure approaching through the mist.

It was Graham Vale.

"What the hell are you doing here?" Victor snapped, his calm veneer cracking for the first time.

Graham ignored him, his eyes locked on Jordan. "Whatever he's told you, it's a lie," he said, his voice desperate. "Victor's been pulling the strings all along. He's the one who made Alice disappear."

Victor's laugh was sharp and bitter. "Oh, please. You think anyone's going to believe the screw-up little brother over me?"

Jordan held up a hand, silencing them both. "Enough. I don't care about your sibling rivalry. I care about Alice. Where is she?"

Neither brother answered.

Jordan took a step closer, their voice hard. "One of you knows the truth. Maybe both of you. But I promise you this: I will find out. And when I do, it won't matter how rich or powerful you are."

Victor's smirk returned, but there was a flicker of unease in his eyes. Graham looked away, guilt written all over his face.

Jordan turned and walked away, their heart pounding.

Back at the Apartment

Jordan barely made it through the door before collapsing onto the couch, their mind racing.

Victor's words replayed in their head: *She underestimated me.*

Graham's desperate plea: *He's the one who made Alice disappear.*

And then there was the photograph, still sitting on their desk, its single word taunting them: *Leverage.*

They pulled out their phone and dialed a number they hadn't called in years.

"I need a favor," Jordan said when the line connected. "And it's going to cost you."

The voice on the other end sighed. "This is about the Vales, isn't it?"

Jordan hesitated, their jaw tightening. "I'm getting too close to something big. And I need backup."

The voice was silent for a moment before replying. "You're playing with fire, Jordan. But I'll help. Where do we start?"

Jordan's eyes flicked to the photograph again. "With Alice. And with Victor Vale."

Chapter 7: The Cracks Begin to Show

The sun barely pierced through the heavy clouds the next morning, casting the city in shades of gray. It matched Jordan's mood perfectly. After the tense confrontation at the pier, they felt as though they were being pulled in every direction. Victor and Graham had painted two completely different pictures of Alice's disappearance, but neither of them could be trusted.

And Eleanor? The supposedly grieving matriarch hadn't been entirely forthcoming either.

Jordan stared at the photograph on their desk, the word *Leverage* seeming to glow against the backdrop of unanswered questions. The name *Argent Capital* kept resurfacing in their mind, its ghostly presence in both Victor's past and Alice's brief tenure raising far too many red flags to ignore.

Breaking Through the Web

Jordan's contact, an old associate named Sam, had agreed to help untangle the financial labyrinth surrounding Argent Capital. Sam had once been a forensic accountant—a gifted one—before deciding that the pay was better on the other side of the law.

"Argent Capital," Sam muttered over the phone, their fingers clicking rapidly against a keyboard. "Victor Vale's pet project back in the day. It was clean on paper, but I always thought there was something off about it."

"Off how?" Jordan asked.

"For starters, most of its assets were funneled into accounts tied to offshore companies—shell corporations with no real business operations. But here's where it gets interesting: just before the company dissolved, someone transferred a substantial sum of money—seven figures—to an untraceable account."

Jordan leaned forward, gripping the phone tightly. "And Alice was working there when this happened?"

"Not just working," Sam said, their voice sharpening. "She was the one who signed off on the transfer."

Jordan's blood ran cold. "Are you saying Alice embezzled the money?"

"Not necessarily," Sam replied. "But her signature's on the paperwork, so either she was involved, or someone set her up."

Jordan's mind raced. If Alice had discovered something about Victor's financial dealings, it would explain the word *Leverage*. It also explained why Victor might have wanted her out of the picture.

"Send me everything you've got," Jordan said.

"You're walking into a hornet's nest, my friend," Sam warned. "Be careful."

The Vale Mansion: Another Visit

That afternoon, Jordan found themselves once again at the imposing gates of the Vale mansion. The place looked even more foreboding in the pale light, its grandeur overshadowed by the secrets buried within its walls.

This time, they had no intention of leaving without answers.

Eleanor was waiting in the drawing room, her posture regal as always. A porcelain teacup sat untouched on the table beside her.

"Mr. Cross," she said, her tone clipped. "I wasn't expecting you."

"Funny," Jordan replied, dropping into a chair across from her. "I wasn't expecting to find out that Alice was neck-deep in your family's dirty business either."

Eleanor's lips thinned. "I suggest you watch your tone."

"Or what?" Jordan challenged. "You'll have me thrown out? That won't stop me from uncovering the truth."

Eleanor sighed, a sound that was more annoyance than defeat. "What exactly do you think you've uncovered?"

Jordan leaned forward, their gaze unwavering. "Argent Capital. The missing money. Alice's signature on the transfer. It all points to one thing: she knew too much. And someone in this family made sure she couldn't use it against them."

Eleanor's expression remained impassive, but Jordan caught the flicker of something in her eyes—fear, perhaps, or guilt.

"You think Victor killed her," she said finally.

"Didn't he?"

Eleanor shook her head slowly. "Victor is ruthless, yes. But he's not a murderer."

"Then who is?" Jordan demanded.

For the first time, Eleanor hesitated. She glanced toward the door, as if checking to ensure they were alone.

"Victor didn't kill Alice," she said, her voice dropping. "But he might as well have. His schemes—his greed—they set everything in motion. Alice... she was trying to protect herself. That's why she took the money. She wanted to disappear before Victor could ruin her."

Jordan's breath caught. "Are you saying Alice faked her disappearance?"

"I don't know," Eleanor admitted. "All I know is that she was desperate. And desperate people do dangerous things."

The Revelation

As Jordan left the mansion, their head swam with Eleanor's words. If Alice had staged her own disappearance, it meant she could still be alive. But why hadn't she surfaced? And what had she been planning to do with the stolen money?

Back at their apartment, Jordan's phone buzzed again—another unlisted number.

This time, the voice on the other end was unmistakable.

"I warned you to stop digging," Victor growled. "Now it's too late."

Before Jordan could respond, the line went dead.

Minutes later, their apartment lights flickered, and the faint sound of footsteps echoed from the hallway outside. Jordan's heart raced as they grabbed the closest thing to a weapon—a heavy metal lamp—and approached the door.

When they flung it open, no one was there. But taped to the door was another envelope.

Inside was a single piece of paper, with four chilling words scrawled across it:

Stay out of this.

And beneath it, a photograph of Jordan—taken from the pier the night before.

Chapter 8: The Echo of the Missing

The photograph of Jordan, taken at the pier, sent a chill through their body. Someone was watching them—closer than they realized, closer than they'd anticipated. Whoever it was, they were skilled enough to get this close unnoticed.

But the photograph was more than a warning. It was a challenge.

Jordan's eyes went back to the grainy image of the pier, studying every detail. Their own silhouette was faintly visible in the corner of the frame, and behind it, the shadows of the old shipping containers loomed large. One shadow stood out—a figure partially obscured, as if deliberately avoiding the light.

Flipping the photograph over, Jordan noticed a faint smudge in the corner, barely legible: *36M-472.*

A number. Or was it a code?

Jordan grabbed their laptop, typing the string into a search engine. Nothing. Next, they tried combinations with keywords like *pier, cargo,* and *shipments.*

Finally, it clicked. The number was part of a container ID, tied to a shipping manifest.

The Hunt Begins

The manifest belonged to an old logistics company, one of many that had leased space at the pier before the port fell into disrepair. Jordan followed the breadcrumb trail, hacking into archived records and tracing shipments.

The trail led them to a warehouse on the city's outskirts, registered under yet another shell corporation. It had been inactive for years—no reported activity, no lights, no maintenance.

It was the kind of place no one would look for a missing person.

The Warehouse

The drive to the warehouse was tense, every streetlight and passing car amplifying Jordan's unease. They parked a block away and approached on foot, keeping to the shadows. The warehouse loomed like a giant tomb, its windows boarded up and its massive doors chained shut.

Jordan circled the building, searching for a way in. They found it in the form of a side door, the padlock rusted and brittle. A few hits with a crowbar—borrowed from their trunk—was all it took to break it.

Inside, the air was thick with the smell of mildew and dust. Rows of crates stretched into the darkness, their labels faded and peeling.

Jordan's flashlight cut through the gloom, illuminating a path deeper into the building. Every creak of the floorboards, every distant rustle of movement set their nerves on edge.

And then, they saw it: container 36M-472, its massive steel doors slightly ajar.

Inside the Container

Jordan hesitated, their heart pounding as they pushed the doors open. The interior was sparse—just a single desk, a chair, and a series of papers pinned to the walls.

The photographs were the first thing Jordan noticed. Dozens of them, all of Alice. Some were candid shots—Alice laughing at a café, walking through a park—while others were unsettlingly intimate, taken through windows or across streets.

In the center of the desk was a journal, its leather cover worn and cracked. Jordan opened it carefully, flipping through its pages.

The entries were written in Alice's hand, her sharp, elegant script unmistakable.

Alice's Journal

August 14

I've underestimated Victor. He knows what I've found, and he won't stop until he silences me. I need to get out before it's too late.

September 2

I've secured the money. It's not enough, but it will have to do. They'll notice soon, but by the time they connect the dots, I'll be gone.

September 15

I can't trust anyone. Not Victor, not Lila, not even Graham. They're all too entangled in this mess.

September 20

I've made arrangements. If something happens to me, the truth will come out. But I can't let them win.

The final entry was dated just two days before Alice's disappearance:

October 3

He's coming for me. I don't know how much time I have left, but I won't let him destroy me. Not without a fight.

Jordan sat back, their mind spinning. Alice had known she was in danger, but she hadn't been running blind. She'd made plans.

The truth was out there, somewhere. And it was bigger than they'd imagined.

An Unwelcome Guest

Jordan's thoughts were interrupted by the sound of footsteps echoing through the warehouse. They froze, every muscle tensing as the steps grew louder.

Quickly, they grabbed the journal and slipped behind a stack of crates, their flashlight turned off.

The footsteps stopped near the container. Jordan peeked out from their hiding spot, their breath catching when they saw who it was.

Victor.

He stood in the doorway of the container, his expression cold as he surveyed the room. His eyes lingered on the desk, narrowing when he noticed the journal was missing.

"I know you're here, Jordan," he called out, his voice calm but laced with menace. "You've made a grave mistake coming here."

Jordan's grip tightened on the journal. They had to get out, but the only exit was blocked by Victor.

"You think you're clever," Victor continued, stepping further into the container. "But you don't understand what you're dealing with. Alice was playing with fire, and it got her burned. Do you really want to meet the same fate?"

Jordan's mind raced. If they stayed hidden, Victor would find them eventually. If they ran, they'd have to move fast and make it count.

The Escape

Before Victor could advance further, Jordan flung the journal as a distraction. The leather-bound book struck the ground with a thud, and Victor spun toward the sound.

Using the momentary diversion, Jordan bolted from their hiding spot, sprinting toward the side door.

"Stop!" Victor shouted, his voice echoing through the warehouse.

Jordan didn't look back. They burst through the door and into the night, their feet pounding against the pavement as they ran for their car.

Behind them, Victor's footsteps grew fainter, but his final words rang in their ears:

"You can't run forever!"

Back at the Apartment

Safe inside, Jordan locked every door and window before collapsing onto the couch. The journal sat on the coffee table, its worn cover a silent reminder of how close they'd come to being caught.

Flipping through its pages again, Jordan's eyes fell on a scribbled note tucked into the back cover.

It was an address.

A flicker of hope ignited in their chest. Could this be where Alice had planned to hide? Or was it something else entirely?

Jordan knew one thing for sure: the next step in their search would either bring them closer to Alice—or put them in even greater danger.

Chapter 9: The Hidden Address

The address on the piece of paper burned in Jordan's hand, its significance growing with every passing moment. The warehouse had been a dead end, but this address—tucked quietly in the back of Alice's journal—felt like the last thread in a rapidly unraveling web.

They sat at their kitchen table, staring at the crumpled paper. It was a residential address, tucked into a sleepy part of the city—a quiet neighborhood of modest homes, away from the flash of high-rise buildings and the bustle of downtown. A place where secrets could hide in plain sight.

Jordan knew they couldn't wait any longer. Every minute they delayed brought them closer to losing Alice forever—or worse.

The Drive to the Address

The address led them to an old neighborhood, one that hadn't seen much change in decades. The houses were small, with overgrown lawns and peeling paint, but there was a quiet beauty to the place, a sort of peaceful anonymity. But beneath that calm exterior, Jordan felt the weight of something darker waiting to be uncovered.

They parked a few blocks away, blending in with the sparse traffic. The street was quiet, too quiet. The kind of quiet that felt like it was holding its breath.

Jordan stepped out of the car and adjusted the strap of their bag. They glanced around, feeling as though they were being watched. The hairs on the back of their neck prickled with unease. But they couldn't stop now.

They followed the address to the end of the street, where a small, unassuming house sat at the corner. The windows were dark, and the front door was slightly ajar.

Jordan's heart skipped. It was exactly the kind of place someone would go to hide—forgotten by the world, away from prying eyes.

Entering the House

Taking a deep breath, Jordan pushed the door open, the hinges creaking in protest. The air inside smelled stale, untouched. Dust covered the furniture, and old newspapers were strewn across the floor, but nothing seemed to indicate that anyone had been here recently.

But something was off. The silence was too complete, the stillness too heavy.

Jordan stepped further inside, the floorboards groaning underfoot. They moved through the house cautiously, eyes scanning every corner. In the living room, an old-fashioned lamp sat on a side table, its bulb unlit. Across the room, a faded painting hung crookedly on the wall.

Then, they saw it. A small, locked box sitting on a table near the window. Its metallic surface was scratched, as though it had been moved or disturbed in a hurry.

The box had a keyhole, and despite everything, Jordan felt a flicker of hope. Could this be the key to understanding everything? Could it be Alice's secret?

The Box

Jordan knelt down and carefully examined the box. The keyhole seemed simple enough, but without the key, it would be useless. They scanned the room for any sign of it. That's when they noticed a small drawer underneath the table. It was slightly ajar, as if someone had hastily opened it and forgotten to close it fully.

Opening the drawer, Jordan's pulse quickened when they saw what lay inside: a small metal key, just the right size for the lock on the box.

With steady hands, they took the key and walked back to the box. As they inserted the key into the lock, they could feel their heart pounding in their chest. This could be the moment where everything changed.

The lock clicked open.

What Was Inside

Inside the box was a stack of papers—documents, photographs, and something else that immediately caught Jordan's eye: a letter.

They picked it up and scanned the first few lines. It was addressed to someone named *Lila Vale*, written in Alice's neat handwriting.

Lila,

I don't know how much longer I have. The truth is, I've been watching Victor for a long time, and I know what he's capable of. I've seen the way he manipulates people, the way he makes everything bend to his will.

But I've also seen the cracks in his armor, and I think I can use that against him. There's a part of me that hopes I'm wrong, that he won't come for me. But I can't take that chance anymore.

I need you to know that if something happens to me, you need to take action. There are people who know about the money, about what I've done. They're all tied to the Vale fortune, and they'll do anything to protect it. But there's something else—something bigger than money. If I disappear, Victor won't just have control of the family's wealth. He'll control everything.

I'm running out of time. If you can, get out. Get away from him before it's too late.

—A

Jordan's breath caught in their throat. The letter was clear: Alice had known that Victor was a threat long before she disappeared. She had been trying to warn someone—maybe Lila, maybe someone else—about what Victor was planning.

The Hidden Truth

Jordan's hands trembled as they went through the rest of the papers. Among them, there were several photos of Victor and Alice together—taken at different events, at different times. But one stood out in particular: a photo of Alice and Victor, standing close, both smiling at the camera. But there was something unsettling about the picture—a strange familiarity between them, something beyond just a family connection.

They flipped through more pages, finding a series of financial records linked to Argent Capital—records Alice had apparently taken as leverage against Victor. There were other names mentioned in the documents—names Jordan didn't recognize at first, but they felt significant.

But then, one name stood out—*Lila Vale*.

Lila Vale: The Key to Everything?

Jordan's mind raced. Lila Vale had been one of the family's most reclusive members, someone who had disappeared from public view long ago. No one ever talked about her, and now, Jordan was starting to see why.

Alice had been in contact with Lila before her disappearance. Was Lila part of the conspiracy? Or was she someone Alice had planned to turn to for help?

A Threat at the Door

Suddenly, a sound echoed from outside the house. Footsteps.

Jordan's blood ran cold. Someone was coming. They had to leave—and fast. But as they turned to leave, they saw something that froze them in place.

A shadow moved across the window, a figure standing just outside the door.

The Confrontation

Before they could react, the door creaked open, and standing in the doorway was none other than **Victor Vale.**

"You're really digging, aren't you, Jordan?" His voice was low, menacing. "You should've stayed out of this. Now, you've put yourself in a position you can't escape from."

Jordan's hand clenched around the papers in their grip. "I'm not going anywhere until I have the truth."

Victor's smile was cold. "The truth? There's no truth here. Just a tangled web of lies. You think you can win against me? You can't. I own this city. I own everything. Including you."

The Final Choice

The walls were closing in on Jordan, and it felt like there was nowhere left to turn. Victor was relentless. He was powerful. But the truth—Alice's truth—was slipping through his fingers, and Jordan had it in their grasp.

"Get out of my way, Victor," Jordan said, their voice steady.

Victor stepped forward. "Make me."

Chapter 10: The Battle of Wits

Victor stood at the threshold, his eyes cold as they locked onto Jordan. Every inch of his presence exuded control, the kind that came with years of manipulating people, bending them to his will. But Jordan wasn't backing down.

"I'm not afraid of you," Jordan said, their voice steady despite the pounding in their chest. "I have what I need. I know what you've done, Victor."

Victor's lips curled into a tight smile. "You think you know me? You think a few papers and photographs are going to change anything?"

Jordan's fingers tightened around the documents in their hands, the pieces of the puzzle that had been slowly falling into place. "I know what you're hiding. The money, the manipulation. You've been pulling the strings behind everything, controlling people from the shadows. But your time's up."

The Power Play

Victor stepped into the room, the door creaking behind him. His footsteps were deliberate, each one echoing as he moved closer. Jordan's heart raced, but they refused to retreat.

"You really have no idea what you're dealing with, do you?" Victor's voice was low, dripping with disdain. "The Vale family didn't build an empire by playing fair. It's about power, Jordan. Power over people, power over information. And you—" He paused, his gaze sharpening. "You're just a pawn. You always have been."

Jordan took a step back, raising their chin defiantly. "Maybe. But even pawns can win the game."

A Dangerous Game

Victor's smirk faded, and for the first time, a flicker of anger crossed his face. "You don't know what you're about to unleash. Alice knew it, too. That's why she's gone. And if you're not careful, you'll end up just like her—disappeared, erased."

The weight of his words hung in the air, like a shadow closing in. But Jordan didn't flinch. They'd come too far to turn back now.

"I'm not afraid of you," Jordan repeated. "I'll expose you. Everything you've done. All of it. And if I go down, I'll take you with me."

Victor's smile returned, but it was more menacing now, a look of cold amusement. "You really think I'd let that happen?" He reached into his coat pocket and pulled out a small, sleek phone, unlocking it with a quick swipe. "I don't need to lift a finger to silence you. I have people everywhere. All I need to do is call one number, and your little search ends. Alice's search ends."

He raised the phone, tapping it as he spoke. "One call, Jordan. That's all it'll take. Do you really want to test me?"

The Call

The words stung, but they only steeled Jordan's resolve. They couldn't back down now, not when they were so close.

"No one controls me," Jordan said, their voice calm but firm. "You've made one mistake, Victor. You underestimated me."

The room fell into a tense silence. Victor's fingers hovered over the phone, but something in Jordan's eyes seemed to give him pause. It wasn't fear—no, it was something else. The edge of desperation, maybe. Or determination.

"Don't be foolish," Victor said, a thin thread of warning in his tone. "I know you think you're playing a clever game, but I've already won."

Jordan glanced at the phone in his hand, then to the papers clenched in theirs. There was a way out of this—a way to take control, to shift the odds in their favor.

They'd learned enough to know that Victor's empire, no matter how well-guarded, had cracks. There was a way to expose the truth, even if it meant using his own game against him.

A Dangerous Decision

Without warning, Jordan made their move. In one swift motion, they lunged forward, swiping the phone from Victor's hand. He staggered back in surprise, his grip loosening just enough for Jordan to seize the device.

For a split second, Victor's eyes flashed with rage. But Jordan didn't hesitate. They tossed the phone to the side, far enough that Victor couldn't grab it easily. Then, with a calculated calmness, they picked up the journal and held it up in front of him.

"You're wrong about one thing, Victor," Jordan said, the words carrying weight. "You think you control everything, but you don't. I've already made sure your dirty little secrets are in the hands of people who can use them. I've sent them to the press, to the ones who can expose you. It's only a matter of time before your empire crumbles."

Victor's eyes widened, his face twisting into an expression of disbelief. "You wouldn't dare. No one would believe you."

Jordan held their ground. "I've got copies of everything. The financial records. The photographs. The letters from Alice. You'll be finished."

Victor's Final Gamble

Victor's expression hardened as his mind raced. For a moment, it seemed as though he was going to charge at Jordan, to wrest the journal from their hands, but then something changed in his eyes. A flicker of calculation.

"You think you've won?" Victor's voice was cold, calculated. "You really think you've outsmarted me? There's more at play here than you realize, Jordan."

Jordan's brow furrowed. "What do you mean?"

Victor's lips curled into a thin, mocking smile. "You've just made a bigger mistake than you know. You've dug too deep, and now you're too entangled. There's no way out for you."

The Twist

Suddenly, the door to the house slammed open with a deafening crash, and Jordan whipped around to see several figures entering. They weren't alone.

Behind them, two men in dark suits stepped forward, their expressions hard and unyielding.

Victor stood up straighter, the cold smile returning. "I told you, Jordan. I own everything."

The men in suits advanced, and before Jordan could react, one of them reached forward and grabbed them by the arm. The other moved swiftly to secure the journal.

"No," Jordan growled, pulling away. "You don't get to do this."

But it was too late. The man with the journal quickly stuffed it into his jacket pocket, and the other tightened his grip on Jordan's arm, pulling them toward the door.

Victor followed, his voice taunting. "You're mine now. You should've known better than to mess with the Vale family."

The Cliffhanger

As Jordan struggled against the grip of the men, their thoughts raced. There was no way they could let Victor get away with this, not after everything they'd uncovered. But now they were outnumbered, and without the journal, it seemed like everything was slipping through their fingers.

This was far from over. The fight for the truth wasn't just about exposure anymore. It was about survival.

The men shoved Jordan into the back of a car, the door slamming shut behind them. The engine roared to life, and the car sped off into the night.

Jordan's thoughts were racing faster than the car. They weren't out of the fight yet.

This wasn't the end.

Chapter 11: A Desperate Escape

The car sped through the dimly lit streets, its engine roaring like an animal hunting in the night. The men in suits were silent, their expressions unreadable, their grip on Jordan tight. With every turn, every bump, Jordan's mind raced. There was no doubt anymore—Victor was playing for keeps. This wasn't just about keeping secrets anymore; it was about silencing them for good.

Jordan glanced out of the window, noting the rapid change in scenery. The urban skyline had been replaced by dense trees and darkened roads. It was clear they were being taken to a place far from civilization—a place where no one would hear them scream.

The pressure of the situation was suffocating. The journal was gone. The papers, the photographs, the evidence they'd gathered—all of it had been stripped away. For a moment, the weight of failure settled in their chest like lead.

But only for a moment.

The Fire of Determination

Jordan's breath slowed. *This wasn't the end.*

They couldn't afford to break now. They had come too far, learned too much. Victor thought he had them cornered, but Jordan wasn't just going to sit back and let the man win. The truth wasn't in the hands of paper—it was in their mind, in their ability to think their way out of impossible situations.

Their eyes scanned the car, looking for an opportunity. The back seat was cramped, but they noticed the small details: the way the light flickered, the position of the rearview mirror, and the fact that one of the men was tapping his fingers nervously against his thigh.

Jordan had to act fast.

The Plan

With swift precision, Jordan shifted their weight and leaned toward the door. In a split-second decision, they reached for the door handle, jerking it with all their strength.

The door flew open, but before they could make a run for it, the man beside them reacted, grabbing their arm in a vice-like grip.

"No! Stay in the car!" he shouted.

But Jordan wasn't going to give up so easily. They twisted their body, using the man's momentum against him. With a desperate grunt, they elbowed him hard in the stomach, catching him off-guard. He let out a sharp gasp, loosening his grip for just a fraction of a second. That was enough.

Jordan wrenched their arm free and kicked the door wide open. Adrenaline surged through their body, and before the other man could react, they were running—fast, determined, and free.

Into the Dark

The night air hit Jordan like a wall, but they didn't stop to catch their breath. The forest loomed ahead, dark and dense, but it was the only way forward. They ran, pushing their body past its limits, ignoring the sharp pain in their legs as they sprinted into the trees.

Behind them, the men shouted, but Jordan didn't dare look back. The car's headlights faded into the distance, swallowed by the dark expanse of the woods. They needed to find shelter, a place to regroup, and most importantly, they needed to get out of this alive.

The Safe Haven

After what felt like hours, Jordan stumbled into a small clearing. Their lungs burned, their legs felt like lead, but they kept moving. They needed a plan. The city was too far away, and Victor's influence reached everywhere. But somewhere in their mind, the name *Lila Vale* echoed—one name that could still hold the key to everything.

Lila was an enigma, a ghost from the past, someone who might know the secrets that could bring Victor down. If Alice had trusted Lila, maybe Jordan could, too. But first, they needed to figure out how to contact her.

A Secret Connection

In the clearing, Jordan finally stopped, their chest heaving as they sank to their knees, exhausted but alive. There, under the light of a dimming moon, they pulled out the last remaining resource—the piece of paper from Alice's journal with Lila's name on it.

Jordan hadn't seen Lila in years, but they remembered one important detail: the number Alice had written in the margins, a number that was supposedly Lila's contact.

It was a long shot, but it was all Jordan had left. With trembling hands, they took out their phone and dialed the number, praying it was still active.

Lila Vale

The phone rang three times before a voice picked up on the other end.

"Hello?" It was a woman's voice, calm and controlled, yet there was an underlying tension.

"This is Jordan," they said quickly, the words tumbling out. "I need to talk to you. It's about Alice. I know what Victor's been hiding, and I—"

"Wait," the voice interrupted, a slight tremor now audible. "What do you know? Who are you?"

Jordan's pulse quickened. "I'm a friend of Alice's. She's gone missing. I found her journal. I have proof of what Victor's doing. I need your help."

There was a long silence on the other end. The woman seemed to be considering something, weighing her options.

Finally, she spoke again, her voice resolute. "Meet me at the old warehouse on 5th and Morrow Street in two hours. Don't be late. And don't trust anyone but me."

The line went dead before Jordan could respond.

A Race Against Time

The phone slipped from Jordan's hand as they tried to steady their racing heart. *Old warehouse, 5th and Morrow.* They had no time to waste. If they were going to survive this, they had to make it there—and fast.

But they couldn't shake the feeling that they were walking into a trap. Victor wouldn't give up so easily. He knew how to play this game, and if Lila was involved, there was no telling which side she was really on.

Jordan had to be smart. They had to be quick.

With only one chance to make this work, they picked up their pace, heading towards the rendezvous point. Time was ticking. The truth was still out there, but every minute they wasted brought them closer to danger.

The Tension Builds

As Jordan made their way to the meeting spot, the tension built to a boiling point. Every shadow seemed to move, every rustle in the trees sent a wave of dread through them.

Was Lila really on their side? Or was this all part of Victor's game? Would they finally get the answers they needed—or would this be the last move in a game they couldn't win?

The warehouse loomed ahead, a dark and looming structure against the night sky. Jordan didn't stop, but their heart pounded faster, knowing that whatever happened next would determine everything.

The Cliffhanger

Jordan reached the old warehouse, but as they approached the entrance, they froze. A figure emerged from the shadows—a familiar figure wearing a long coat, standing in the doorway.

It was Lila. But something about her posture was off, and as she turned to face Jordan, a cold smile spread across her lips.

"I knew you'd come," she said. "But you should've stayed away."

Chapter 12: The Betrayal

Jordan's heart hammered against their chest as they stood frozen in front of the warehouse. Lila's silhouette was barely visible, but the way she stood—calm, calculating, almost as if waiting for something—sent a chill down Jordan's spine. Something was wrong. Lila wasn't the ally they had hoped for.

"I knew you'd come," Lila said, her voice cool and almost detached. "But you should've stayed away."

Jordan's mind raced. The words felt like a warning, not a greeting. "Lila, I—"

"You think you're the first one to come looking for answers?" Lila interrupted, stepping into the dim light. Her coat fluttered slightly in the wind, and Jordan saw her eyes—sharp, calculating—like they were sizing them up, dissecting every move. "You have no idea what you're dealing with."

"I don't know what's going on, but I'm trying to fix it," Jordan said, trying to steady their voice. "I need to know about Victor. About Alice. What did he do to her?"

Lila smirked, a dark, almost predatory expression. "You really think Victor did this to Alice? You think he's the only one with blood on his hands?" She took a step closer, her movements slow but deliberate. "Let me tell you something, Jordan. Alice was just the beginning."

Jordan's throat tightened. "What do you mean? What are you saying?"

Lila's eyes gleamed with a sharp, unsettling intensity. "You've been running around, chasing shadows, digging into things you don't understand. You think you can expose Victor? You think you can take down the Vale family?" Her laugh was short, almost mocking. "You're not even close."

The pieces of the puzzle started to fall into place, but not in the way Jordan had expected. Their stomach twisted as the realization hit:

Lila wasn't here to help them. She was here to control them—or destroy them.

The Dark Revelation

Jordan took a step back, a cold sweat forming on their skin. "You're working with him, aren't you?"

Lila didn't flinch. "I'm working for the truth. You think this is just about Victor? No. There's more at play here, Jordan. A lot more."

The wind howled through the cracks in the warehouse, adding to the eerie silence. Jordan felt the weight of Lila's words settle heavily on them. "What do you mean? What more is there?"

Lila leaned in slightly, her voice dropping to a whisper. "Alice wasn't the only one digging for answers. She stumbled onto something far bigger than you could imagine. Something Victor doesn't want anyone to find." She paused, then said, her voice colder than ever, "But you've already found it. Haven't you?"

Jordan swallowed hard. "Found what?"

Lila's smile widened, but it wasn't a friendly smile. It was a smile full of secrets, full of knowing. "The Vale family has more than just money and power. They have something much darker. And you, Jordan, have already become part of that darkness. Whether you want to or not."

The Trap

Before Jordan could react, the sharp sound of footsteps echoed from behind. They turned just in time to see two more figures emerge from the shadows, their faces obscured by the darkness but their intent clear. They were here to make sure Jordan didn't leave. Lila's grin grew.

"You should've stayed away, Jordan," she repeated, her voice almost pitying now. "You've become a liability."

The two figures moved quickly, closing in on Jordan, who backed up instinctively, their eyes darting around the warehouse for an escape. There was nowhere to run.

"I should've known," Jordan muttered under their breath. "You were never going to help me."

Lila sighed, the slightest hint of disappointment in her voice. "I wanted to, really. But this isn't a game you can win. Not anymore. Now you're in it whether you like it or not."

The figures stepped closer, one of them pulling out a small, sleek device—a tracker. Jordan's heart skipped a beat. They were marking them. Their every move would be tracked now.

Desperation surged through them. There had to be a way out. They couldn't let themselves get captured again—not when they were so close.

The Unexpected Ally

Just as one of the figures lunged to grab Jordan, a sudden crash echoed through the warehouse. A loud bang, followed by the shattering of glass, filled the air. The figures froze for a moment, confusion flashing across their faces.

And then, from the far side of the warehouse, a familiar voice rang out.

"Let them go."

It was **Alice.**

No, it wasn't Alice. The voice, while eerily similar, carried a different edge—one of authority, of command.

The figures immediately turned toward the voice, their eyes scanning the shadows. A figure stepped forward, tall and cloaked in dark clothing, moving with a predatory grace. As the figure stepped into the light, Jordan's eyes widened in disbelief.

Standing before them was **Nash Winters**, an old associate of Alice's—someone Jordan had never fully trusted, but had never thought capable of this.

The Twist

"You," Jordan whispered, taken aback.

Nash's face was expressionless, but there was a coldness in his eyes that Jordan had never seen before. "I was hoping you'd figure it out," he said, his voice low. "I had to make sure you didn't get yourself killed. But now, it seems we've run out of time."

Lila's expression twisted in fury. "You—"

"I did what had to be done, Lila," Nash interrupted, his voice cold, unforgiving. "And now we finish what Alice started. I've been watching you. I've been watching Victor. And we'll take them all down, one by one."

The Final Stand

Jordan could hardly comprehend the shift in the room. One moment, they were facing betrayal from every corner, and now, Nash was offering them a way out—or at least a way to fight back.

Lila's face darkened, her expression turning to one of fierce defiance. "You think you can just waltz in here and—"

"No, Lila," Nash cut in, his voice like steel. "This ends now."

The tension in the warehouse was palpable, the air thick with uncertainty. Jordan felt like they were caught in a web of lies and power struggles, and they had no idea who to trust. But one thing was clear: the game had changed.

The truth was finally within reach. But the cost of exposing it? Jordan wasn't sure if they could survive it.

The Cliffhanger

With a sudden motion, Nash gestured to the other figures, who swiftly moved into position, surrounding Lila and her men. "We don't have time for this," Nash said. "You want to fight, Lila? Then we'll fight. But you don't get to control this anymore."

Lila sneered, but there was a hint of fear in her eyes. She wasn't as confident as she had been moments ago. The pieces were finally shifting.

Jordan's gaze flickered between Lila and Nash, unsure whether they should feel relieved or more terrified than ever.

They had no choice now. They had to go with Nash. And they had to hope, against all odds, that this would lead them to the truth.

Chapter 13: Unraveling the Web

The air inside the warehouse felt suffocating. It was as if the walls themselves had closed in, tightening around Jordan, Lila, and Nash. The sounds of their breathing echoed, punctuated only by the occasional creaks of the structure under the weight of time.

Jordan stood, frozen, trying to process the new reality. Nash Winters—an enigma, an old ally, someone who had worked with Alice in the shadows of Victor's empire—was now here, standing between them and Lila, the very woman who had made it clear she was no friend.

Lila was the first to break the silence. She laughed, a low, mocking sound that reverberated off the cold concrete walls. "You really think you've won, Nash? That *this*—" she gestured toward the figures surrounding her, "—will change anything?"

Nash didn't flinch. He stood still, his eyes cold, calculating. "I'm not here for you, Lila. I'm here to make sure this ends. Once and for all."

Jordan's heart was pounding. What was happening? Nash, someone they had only heard about through Alice's fragmented stories, was now standing as their only possible ally. But could they trust him? Or was he part of the larger game all along?

The Unfolding Plan

"Who's *we*, Nash?" Jordan finally managed, their voice strained. "And what do you mean, 'make sure this ends'?"

Nash's face softened, just a fraction, as if deciding whether to share the whole truth. "Alice didn't die just because Victor wanted her out of the way. She was too close to uncovering something—something much bigger than you can imagine. The Vale family isn't just rich; they've been pulling strings for decades, orchestrating things from behind the scenes.

You, Jordan, you were caught in the middle of it all. You don't even know the half of it."

Jordan's mind raced, trying to process his words. *Too close to uncovering something. Caught in the middle.* It felt like a storm was gathering around them, and they were standing at its epicenter.

"You need to trust me," Nash continued. "You're not just fighting for Alice's justice. You're fighting for something that could bring everything down—the Vale family, Victor's empire, the entire network of power he's created. But we don't have much time."

Lila sneered, stepping forward. "Do you really think you can stop Victor? You're nothing more than a piece in his game, Nash. And Jordan, too. You're both expendable."

Her words hit harder than Jordan expected. It wasn't just about taking down a powerful man—it was about dismantling a dynasty, a legacy of manipulation and control. *But how?* How could they take on something that had been built over generations?

The Turning Point

A sharp noise sliced through the tension. One of Lila's men, who had been standing near the back of the room, suddenly stepped forward, holding a device in his hand. Jordan's eyes widened. It was a signal jammer.

"Lila, don't—" Nash's voice rose, but it was too late.

The man pressed a button, and the once steady hum of the warehouse's lights flickered and went out, plunging them into darkness. The low buzz of the emergency lights soon followed, casting long shadows across the room. Jordan's pulse quickened. Was this the moment everything unraveled? The moment Victor's people would finally come for them?

The darkness was thick, suffocating. Jordan's mind spun, trying to piece together what was happening. Nash had been working to take Victor down, and now Lila—who had been so confident before—seemed desperate to stop it. Was she afraid?

Suddenly, Nash's voice cut through the silence. "We need to move. Now."

Without hesitation, he grabbed Jordan's arm and pulled them toward a door at the far end of the warehouse. Lila's men hesitated for a second, unsure of what to do, but then the sound of their boots on the floor followed them in hot pursuit.

The Chase

They burst out into the night, the cold air biting at their skin. The streets were eerily empty, the only sound the distant hum of the city. Nash led the way, pulling Jordan through the alleyways, keeping low and fast.

Jordan's thoughts raced. They had barely escaped Lila's trap, but the danger wasn't over. In fact, it had only just begun. Nash seemed to know where he was going, but they had no idea what to expect. Every turn felt like a step deeper into enemy territory.

"Where are we going?" Jordan gasped, struggling to keep up with Nash's long strides.

"There's a safe house," Nash said, his voice tight with urgency. "It's one of the few places where we can regroup. We need to figure out what's next. The truth—everything you want to know—it's inside the Vale network. But we need time. And we need the right resources."

Jordan nodded, their mind still reeling. *Time.* Time for what? To gather evidence? To plan their next move? Or to wait for Victor's inevitable retaliation?

Suddenly, Nash pulled up short, motioning for Jordan to stop. He pressed his back against the wall, listening for movement.

Footsteps.

They weren't alone. More of Lila's men were closing in, and they weren't going to let them go easily.

"Get ready," Nash whispered.

The Final Showdown

The seconds stretched into eternity as the footsteps grew louder, closer. Jordan could feel their heart pounding in their chest. This was it. This was the moment that would define everything.

Nash glanced at Jordan, his face set in grim determination. "We do this now. For Alice. For everyone."

Before Jordan could respond, Nash pulled out a small, sleek pistol from his jacket—no time for hesitation. The footsteps were almost on top of them.

And then the shadows of their pursuers appeared around the corner.

Chapter 14: Into the Abyss

The alley was dark, its shadows heavy with secrets. Jordan's breath was sharp, their legs aching from the mad dash they had just made. Behind them, the sounds of footsteps and hushed voices echoed off the walls—Lila's men were close, but Nash moved like a shadow, his presence almost blending into the night.

They rounded another corner, their pace quickening. Jordan barely had time to catch their breath before Nash pressed them up against a rusted gate. It felt like the world was closing in around them—darkness on all sides, danger at their heels, and a truth so deep it threatened to swallow them whole.

"Stay low," Nash whispered, his voice barely audible over the wind.

Jordan nodded, instinctively crouching lower. Their heart raced. Every fiber of their being screamed for answers. *Who could they trust? Was Nash truly their ally, or was this just another layer of the web Victor had spun around them?*

But there was no time for doubts now.

Nash motioned for them to follow, his hand on the gate's latch. It creaked open, revealing a narrow path that led to a hidden underground garage—a safe house, according to Nash. As they slipped through the gate, Nash pulled it shut with a soft but deliberate motion.

Jordan glanced over their shoulder, half-expecting to see Lila's men right behind them. But the alley was silent.

"For now, we're safe," Nash said, his eyes scanning the surroundings. "But we don't have much time."

A Place to Hide

The garage was dimly lit, filled with the scent of motor oil and old metal. Jordan's mind was a swirl of confusion. They had just barely escaped the clutches of Lila's men, and now, here they were, in some secret hideout, with no idea what Nash's next move was.

Nash headed straight for a set of shelves at the far end of the room. He moved with purpose, his fingers sliding over the surface of the books and boxes, as if he were searching for something specific.

"What are you looking for?" Jordan asked, keeping their voice low.

Nash didn't look up. "I'm looking for something to explain all of this—something that connects the dots." He paused, then added, "This isn't just about the Vale family anymore. It's about something bigger. And you've become part of it. Whether you like it or not."

Jordan swallowed. They didn't want to believe it, but the reality was sinking in. They had stepped into a game they didn't understand, one where the rules kept changing, and their every move seemed to bring more danger.

Suddenly, Nash pulled a small, leather-bound notebook from the shelf. He opened it, flipping through the pages with the precision of someone who had seen them before. His eyes narrowed as he found the right page.

"This is what Alice was working on," he said, his voice steady. "She was tracking everything the Vale family had their hands in—their businesses, their connections, their hidden deals. But it's not just about money. There's something much darker at play here. Something Alice uncovered before she—" He stopped abruptly, his jaw tightening.

Before she died.

Jordan's stomach twisted at the unspoken words. It was still too raw, too painful to think about Alice's death. But they had no choice now but to face the truth, no matter how much it hurt.

The Revelation

Nash set the notebook down on the workbench in front of Jordan, flipping to a page filled with notes, sketches, and names—too many names. Jordan leaned in, trying to make sense of the chaos on the page.

One name stood out: *Victor Vale.*

But it wasn't just the name—it was the symbols beside it, the lines connecting him to several other figures, each one more powerful and dangerous than the last.

"It's not just about Victor," Nash said quietly, as if reading Jordan's mind. "He's the face of the Vale empire, but there are others behind him. People you don't know. People who control everything."

Jordan's pulse quickened. "Who are they?"

Nash looked up, his expression grim. "I don't have all the answers yet, but what I do know is that they're untouchable. They've covered their tracks for decades. The Vale family isn't just powerful—they're *untouchable*. And if we go any further, if we keep digging, we're not just going up against Victor. We're going up against *everyone*."

The weight of Nash's words hit Jordan like a punch to the gut. They had been chasing answers, but what if those answers were more dangerous than they could have imagined?

The Intruder

Before Jordan could process Nash's warning, the sound of a door creaking open interrupted the silence.

Both Nash and Jordan turned toward the sound, instincts flaring. Someone was here.

The figure stepped out of the shadows, and for a split second, Jordan's heart skipped a beat.

It was **Lila.**

But there was something different about her now. She didn't look like the confident woman who had tried to control everything. Instead, she seemed... vulnerable. Her eyes were wide, haunted, and she held her hands up in a gesture of surrender.

"I didn't come here to fight," Lila said, her voice quiet but urgent. "I came here to warn you."

Nash tensed. "Warn us? After everything—"

"I'm not your enemy," Lila interrupted, her gaze flicking between Nash and Jordan. "I never was. But there's more at stake here than you realize. More than any of us can stop alone."

Jordan could hardly believe it. This was the same woman who had tried to kill them not even a few hours ago.

"What are you talking about?" Jordan asked, their voice tight with suspicion.

Lila took a deep breath. "There's a traitor in the Vale family. Someone inside, someone close to Victor, is working against him. And I've been tracking them, trying to get close enough to expose them. But they're too good. They know everything. And they're watching all of us."

The Ultimate Betrayal

Lila's words hit Jordan like a ton of bricks. A traitor? Inside the Vale family? It seemed impossible.

But Nash's expression hardened as he processed the information. "So, you think you can just waltz in here, after everything, and we'll trust you?"

Lila met his gaze, unflinching. "I'm not asking for your trust. But you need to listen. If you don't, Victor will win. He's been playing this game for a long time. And right now, he's got the upper hand."

Nash stayed silent, his eyes narrowed. But Jordan could feel the tension between them. This was a chance—a dangerous one, but a chance nonetheless. If there was a traitor inside the Vale family, it could change everything.

The problem was, who could they trust now?

Chapter 15: Shadows of Deceit

The atmosphere in the hideout was thick with uncertainty. The dim light of a single bulb overhead cast long shadows that seemed to stretch across the room, making every movement feel magnified, every decision more consequential.

Jordan stood at the far end of the room, their eyes locked on Lila. Despite everything—the lies, the manipulation, the threats—there was something about her that felt... different. Was it fear in her eyes? Or guilt? It was hard to tell. But one thing was certain: she wasn't the same confident woman who had tried to kill them just hours ago.

Nash stood opposite her, arms crossed, his gaze fixed on Lila with a mixture of suspicion and wariness.

"I'm not trusting you yet," Nash finally said, breaking the silence. "You've got a lot of explaining to do, Lila. One minute, you're our enemy, the next, you're claiming to be a whistleblower. What's the catch?"

Lila's lips tightened, but she didn't flinch. She met his eyes, her own dark and calculating. "You don't have to trust me. But you need to listen."

Jordan exchanged a glance with Nash. The unease was palpable. Could they trust her? Could they afford not to?

"Who is the traitor?" Jordan asked, their voice steady but laced with urgency. They could feel time slipping away, the weight of Victor's empire bearing down on them.

Lila inhaled deeply, as if the answer was something too dangerous to speak aloud. "Someone close to Victor. Someone in his inner circle. I don't know their identity yet, but I've been tracking them for weeks. They're feeding Victor false information, steering him in the wrong direction—making him paranoid. I've seen the signs. The weird things he's been doing—his sudden movements, his increasing suspicion toward everyone. It's not just power plays. It's manipulation from the inside."

"Manipulation from the inside?" Nash repeated, narrowing his eyes. "That's a hell of an accusation. And you're sure about this?"

Lila nodded, her face grim. "I'm sure. Whoever it is, they're playing a long game. They know every move Victor makes. And they're waiting for the perfect moment to strike."

The Web Tightens

The room seemed to grow smaller as the words hung between them like a heavy fog. For a moment, all Jordan could think about was Alice—the woman they had been so desperate to avenge. Had Alice been onto this same trail? Was this why she had been targeted? Had she been a threat to the inner workings of the Vale empire?

The questions gnawed at Jordan's insides, making it impossible to focus.

"What do you want from us?" Nash's voice broke through the haze of thought, pulling Jordan back into the present. "Why are you telling us this? What's in it for you?"

Lila hesitated before answering, her eyes flickering with something unreadable. "I don't want Victor's empire. I never did. But this game he's playing is dangerous. And if we don't expose the traitor, if we don't take Victor down once and for all, everything will be destroyed. The lives of everyone involved—the ones who are trying to do the right thing—will be meaningless."

Jordan felt a surge of doubt. Could they believe her? Or was this just another move in a much larger game?

"There's a bigger picture here," Lila continued. "Victor is getting reckless. He's starting to turn on the people closest to him. And I'm not just talking about you, Nash. I'm talking about the people he's trusted for years. People who think they're untouchable. He's losing control. And that's when the traitor will strike. When he's vulnerable."

A Moment of Choice

Nash stepped forward, his expression hardening. "And you expect us to just trust you? You expect us to walk straight into the heart of Victor's empire and play into whatever game you're leading?"

Lila's jaw clenched. "No. I expect you to make a choice. There's a moment coming soon when the traitor will act. And if you're not prepared, if you don't know who's on your side, you'll be caught in the crossfire."

For a moment, it felt like the room held its breath. The tension between Nash and Lila was palpable, a quiet storm waiting to explode.

Jordan stepped forward, their mind racing. "We can't let Victor get away with this. We can't let his empire keep running unchecked."

Nash's eyes softened slightly, and for the first time, he seemed to consider Lila's words more deeply. "And what exactly do you propose we do, Lila?"

Lila's face was serious, no trace of the smugness from earlier remaining. "You're going to have to go deeper. Into his circle. Into the people he trusts the most. The traitor is waiting for the right moment to move, but if we can expose them before that happens, we can destroy everything he's built. It's the only way."

Jordan felt a chill run down their spine. What Lila was suggesting wasn't just dangerous—it was a long shot. But it was the only shot they had.

"I don't know if we can trust you," Jordan said, their voice quiet but firm. "But we can't do this alone."

Lila nodded, her eyes meeting Jordan's with an intensity that spoke volumes. "You don't have a choice. None of us do."

The Countdown Begins

As the minutes passed, the weight of the decision pressed on them. Every second counted. The network of betrayal, lies, and power was more complex than any of them had anticipated, and yet, here they were, standing on the edge of a cliff, with no clear way down.

Jordan felt the familiar tension in their chest, the same feeling they'd had when Alice had first asked them to trust her. It was the feeling of standing on the precipice of something big, something that could change everything.

"We need to get to the source," Nash said finally, his tone resolute. "If we're going to do this, we need to go to the heart of the Vale empire. We need to expose the traitor, and we need to do it fast. The longer we wait, the more dangerous this gets."

Lila gave a sharp nod. "You're right. The traitor's patience will run out. We need to move quickly."

Jordan felt the weight of the moment settle over them. They had crossed a line. There was no turning back now.

They were in this—together.

Chapter 16: The Hidden Web

The garage door creaked open with a low, groaning sound, revealing the first traces of dawn peeking over the horizon. The night had passed in a blur of tension, whispered strategies, and uneasy silences. The decision had been made, and there was no turning back now.

Lila stood by the door, her eyes scanning the empty street outside, her movements swift and precise. Nash and Jordan stood off to the side, preparing themselves for the perilous journey ahead. Neither of them had said much since Lila's revelation, but the weight of their shared knowledge hung in the air like a thick fog.

"Are we ready?" Nash's voice broke the silence, sharp and steady, but there was an undercurrent of doubt in his words.

Jordan's hand instinctively tightened around the handle of their bag, the cool leather offering a fleeting sense of comfort in the face of the unknown. "We don't have a choice," they said, meeting his eyes with a quiet resolve. "We have to find the traitor. Expose them. Or we lose everything."

Lila shot them both a glance before stepping out into the early morning light. "This is it. This is our only shot," she said, her tone no longer that of an enemy, but of someone who had chosen to ally themselves in a dangerous game. "We move fast, and we stay quiet. Victor's people will be looking for us. And if they find us, it's over."

Nash grunted in acknowledgment and followed her out, Jordan close behind. The world outside was eerily quiet, the streets bathed in the soft glow of dawn. But the peace was fleeting—an illusion that masked the storm to come.

The City of Secrets

The city loomed before them, its towering buildings casting long, sharp shadows on the streets below. For years, Jordan had navigated these streets, unaware of the undercurrent of danger that ran beneath the surface. But now, with every corner they turned, every alley they passed, the city felt like a maze of secrets waiting to be uncovered.

Lila led them through narrow backstreets, away from the main roads, her steps quick and purposeful. She seemed to know exactly where they were headed, as though she had mapped out every possible escape route. But even with her guidance, Jordan couldn't shake the feeling that they were walking directly into a trap.

"I'm not sure I like this," Nash muttered, glancing over his shoulder. "We're being led by someone we can't trust."

Lila shot him a brief look but didn't respond. Instead, she pressed on, her expression unreadable.

Jordan understood Nash's hesitation. Trusting Lila was dangerous, but what choice did they have? The clues they had gathered pointed to one conclusion: the traitor was still within the Vale empire, and they needed to find them before the traitor found them first.

The Hidden Safe house

They finally reached a building tucked away on the outskirts of the city. The facade was inconspicuous, a plain structure that could have been anyone's home. But Jordan knew better now. This was no ordinary house. It was part of the network that Victor and his allies had built—a safe house that housed secrets, whispers, and shadows.

Lila led them inside, her eyes darting around as if searching for any signs of surveillance. The interior was sparse but functional, with a few pieces of old furniture scattered around the room. A large desk dominated one corner, its surface covered with papers, blueprints, and old maps.

"This is where we get serious," Lila said, gesturing to the table. "I've been tracking the people closest to Victor. The traitor's network is bigger than we thought."

She handed Jordan a stack of photographs, each one showing someone they recognized from Victor's inner circle. But there was something off about them—people standing too close to each other, faces blurred, details hidden in the shadows. It was clear that whoever the traitor was, they had been careful—meticulous.

"We need to figure out who's been leaking information," Lila continued, pointing to the photographs. "These people are the key. If we can find the connection between them, we'll know who the traitor is."

Jordan studied the photographs closely, the names beneath each image becoming more and more familiar. But there was one person who stood out. A familiar face—someone Jordan had once trusted. Someone who had always seemed loyal.

Their heart skipped a beat as the realization dawned.

"This person," Jordan whispered, their finger hovering over one photograph. "They're connected to everything."

Lila turned sharply to look at them. "What do you mean?"

"This person," Jordan repeated, voice barely audible. "They were in charge of securing sensitive information for Victor. They were the one who could have accessed everything."

Nash stepped closer, studying the photo with a frown. "If that's true, it changes everything. We need to find them. Fast."

The Hunt Begins

As the hours passed, they dug deeper into the trail, piecing together fragments of information from their research and the photographs Lila had collected. The more they uncovered, the clearer the pattern became. The traitor wasn't just someone within the Vale family's immediate circle—it was someone with access to the most guarded secrets of their empire.

Lila's phone buzzed, breaking the silence of their investigation. She answered quickly, her voice low and urgent. Jordan couldn't hear the conversation, but from the look on her face, they knew something had changed.

Lila hung up, her eyes dark. "They've moved. The traitor's on the move."

"What do you mean?" Nash demanded, stepping forward. "Where?"

"The city. They're heading toward a meeting point. A place Victor has used in the past," Lila said, her voice clipped. "We need to get there before they do."

Jordan felt their pulse quicken. This was it—the moment they had been waiting for. The traitor was about to make their move, and they had to be there to stop it.

The Final Confrontation

The streets blurred as they raced toward their destination, the weight of their mission pressing down on them with every passing second. The traitor was close, and with each turn they took, the tension in Jordan's chest grew.

They arrived at an old warehouse, its windows dark and silent. A lone car sat outside, its engine running, waiting for someone to arrive.

Lila gave a subtle signal, and the three of them moved in, staying low, keeping to the shadows. They reached the door of the warehouse, and Lila paused, her hand on the handle.

"This is it," she whispered, her voice barely audible. "Stay close. We move together."

Jordan's heart raced. It was time to expose the truth. To finally confront the traitor who had been pulling the strings from the shadows.

But as Lila opened the door, they were met not with a lone figure, but a room full of people—Victor's most trusted allies. And standing at the center of them was none other than—

Chapter 17: Veil of Betrayal

The air in the warehouse was thick with the scent of dust and rust. Jordan's breath quickened as they pressed their back against the cold, concrete wall, listening for any sounds coming from inside. The tension was unbearable. Every muscle in their body was coiled, ready to spring into action.

Lila motioned for silence, her eyes scanning the darkened interior. Nash was beside her, his face hard, but Jordan could see the flicker of uncertainty in his eyes. This wasn't just another mission. This wasn't just about exposing a traitor.

This was personal.

Jordan's mind raced as they crouched low, inching toward the door. They had been so close, so sure that they were about to catch the person who had been undermining everything they had worked for. The person who had been pulling strings, manipulating Victor's empire from within.

Lila paused, her hand on the door handle. "Stay sharp," she whispered.

With a single, decisive push, she swung the door open.

The Warehouse Showdown

Inside, the warehouse was bathed in a dim, flickering light. Shadowy figures moved like ghosts between the stacks of crates and old machinery. A long table stood in the center of the room, cluttered with maps, blueprints, and an array of documents. The scene seemed calm—almost too calm—given the high stakes of their mission.

And then, standing at the head of the table, was the last person Jordan ever expected to see.

"Victor," Jordan muttered under their breath.

The man who had controlled so much of their life, the man who had been their greatest enemy, was standing right in front of them, as calm and collected as ever.

But what froze Jordan's blood wasn't just his presence—it was the way he was speaking to the others. The figures around the table were none other than Victor's inner circle, all of them listening intently to his every word.

Lila tensed beside Jordan, her eyes darting to the shadows where the traitor was supposed to be. "This isn't right," she whispered, her voice tight with anxiety. "They're already here."

Victor's voice broke through the silence. "I've known about the traitor for weeks," he said, his tone casual, but there was an edge to it. "But they underestimated me. They thought they could destroy everything I've built. They thought they could turn my empire against me. But they were wrong."

Jordan's heart skipped a beat. The traitor was already here, and they had walked right into a trap.

The Shocking Truth

Before Jordan could process what was happening, the door behind them slammed shut, and the room seemed to close in. They spun around, eyes wide, only to see several of Victor's loyal guards blocking the exit. There was no way out.

And then, the most unexpected person stepped forward from the shadows: Alice.

Jordan's pulse raced. "Alice? What are you—?"

But Alice's expression was unreadable, her eyes cold and distant. She didn't even flinch at Jordan's voice.

"Alice?" Nash said, his voice cracking with disbelief. "You're the traitor?"

Alice's lips twisted into a tight, mocking smile. "Oh, I'm not the traitor, Nash. I'm the one who's been playing both sides." She turned toward Victor, her gaze meeting his. "He's been so paranoid lately, but I knew I could use that. He never suspected me because he never thought anyone could outsmart him. And now..." She looked back at Jordan and Nash, her smile widening. "Now, everything's going according to plan."

Victor's eyes gleamed with satisfaction as he stepped forward. "Alice has been working for me all along. The traitor you've been chasing? That was just a distraction. She's been feeding you false leads, pulling you into a web of lies."

Jordan's mind reeled. They had been duped. Every move they had made had been manipulated. Every trust they'd extended had been a mistake. They had trusted Alice—the one person they thought was an ally.

The Crossroads

The room felt smaller as the full weight of the betrayal sank in. Alice had been playing both sides. But why? What was her endgame?

Victor leaned against the table, a smug look on his face as he watched the realization hit Jordan and Nash. "You've been pawns in a much bigger game than you realized. Alice and I have been working together for months, feeding you just enough information to keep you on the right track. But now it's time for the final move."

Nash took a step forward, his fists clenched. "You used us. You used Jordan. And for what? To get closer to Victor's power?"

Alice shook her head. "No. To gain control. To make sure I came out on top. You two were never part of the plan. You were just... obstacles."

The room was silent, the tension thick and suffocating. For a moment, it felt like everything had crumbled. The lies, the deception, the trust—they had all been shattered.

Jordan's gaze flickered to Lila, who had been silently watching the scene unfold. Her expression was unreadable, but there was a quiet rage behind her eyes.

"This isn't over," Jordan said, their voice low but full of determination. "We're not going down like this. We still have a chance."

Victor's laugh echoed in the room. "You're not in control here, Jordan. You never were."

The Final Move

Jordan's mind raced. The betrayal was deeper than they had ever anticipated. The game had been rigged from the start, and now they were on the brink of losing everything.

But they weren't ready to give up. Not yet.

In a split second, Jordan made a decision.

"Now!" they shouted.

Without thinking, they lunged forward, grabbing the nearest weapon—one of the abandoned crates—and hurled it toward Victor. The distraction worked, just long enough for Nash to break free from his stunned silence. He grabbed a metal rod and charged forward, aiming for Alice.

Chaos erupted. The sound of clashing metal, grunts, and shouts filled the air as the fight for control began in earnest.

Jordan fought back the fear rising in their chest. There was no turning back now. The final battle had begun.

Chapter 18: The Final Hour

The warehouse had descended into chaos, with every moment feeling like it could be their last. Jordan, Nash, and Lila fought with everything they had, but Victor's loyalists were too numerous, and Alice, who had once been a trusted ally, was an unexpected force. As the dust settled, it became clear: this wasn't just a battle for survival. It was the last play in a dangerous game that had spiraled far beyond their initial plan.

The Clash with Alice

The adrenaline surged through Jordan's veins as they blocked Alice's attack, barely able to maintain their balance as they retreated back into the shadows of the warehouse. Alice's face twisted in anger, her expression barely human.

"You really thought you could beat me?" Alice taunted, her eyes gleaming with triumph. "You were never meant to win, Jordan. I've been playing you from the beginning. I *am* the one in control."

Jordan's heart hammered in their chest. But they refused to be intimidated. They had come too far to back down now. With a fierce determination, Jordan steadied their breath, analyzing the room.

Lila, still reeling from the shock of Alice's betrayal, stood by Jordan's side, ready to fight. But it was Nash who made the first move, charging forward with a furious roar. He swung a metal rod, narrowly missing Alice, who nimbly ducked and countered with a swift strike to Nash's side. The impact sent him stumbling, but his resolve never wavered.

"You're nothing but a puppet, Alice!" Nash shouted, his voice full of venom. "Victor never cared about you. You were just his tool, like the rest of us!"

Alice's eyes flickered with something—regret, fear, or maybe a memory of what she once was—but it was quickly masked by the coldness that had consumed her. "You're wrong, Nash. I've always been in control. I've always known how to play the game. And now, it's over."

Victor's True Motivation

As Alice's words hung in the air, Victor's voice interrupted, colder than before. He stepped forward from the shadows, his presence overpowering. "You were a tool, Alice. Nothing more. Just like all of you."

Jordan froze as Victor's cold eyes locked onto theirs. For a moment, time seemed to stand still, and they realized the truth: they had never been dealing with just a man. Victor's empire wasn't just about money or power—it was about something much darker. He had never cared about them, only about control. He was a master manipulator, and they had been his puppets all along.

"You thought you were fighting for something," Victor continued, his voice smooth. "But you were never really fighting me. You were fighting yourselves. You're all expendable. I'm the one who holds the real power."

Jordan's stomach churned, the weight of Victor's words sinking in. It wasn't just about exposing a traitor—it was about surviving the twisted game he had created.

But there was still one piece of the puzzle left.

The Revelation: The True Traitor

Just as things seemed to be spiraling out of control, Lila's voice broke through. "Wait. There's more. Victor—you're wrong."

All eyes turned to her. Her face was pale, but her voice was steady. "The true traitor isn't just one person. It's all of us. Every one of us has been complicit in the lies, in the games we've played."

Lila took a deep breath, her eyes locking with Jordan's. "I wasn't just trying to survive. I was trying to end the cycle. I know what Victor's after, and I know how to stop it."

A silence fell over the room. Even Victor seemed momentarily stunned, but he quickly regained his composure.

"Enough," he snapped. "You're wasting time. There is no stopping me. This is my game."

Lila's eyes flashed with determination. "That's where you're wrong. I know where your weakness is. It's not your empire. It's not your power. It's your obsession with control. You've underestimated us."

The truth hit them all like a hammer. Victor had been consumed by his need to control everything—every person, every move, every outcome. But in his obsession, he had failed to recognize that his empire was built on lies, and that was the foundation that would crumble.

The Final Confrontation: Breaking the Cycle

A surge of power and clarity washed over Jordan. They realized that to stop Victor, they had to break free from the cycle of manipulation and deceit. They couldn't just fight Victor—they had to dismantle his hold over everyone in the room.

In a swift move, Jordan grabbed the table where the documents lay, slamming it into the ground. "This isn't just about us anymore. This is about everything we've lost—our freedom, our lives. And we're taking it back."

Nash and Lila, now fully aligned, stepped forward, joining Jordan in defiance. The three of them stood together, ready to face the final battle. They weren't just fighting for survival anymore—they were fighting for their lives, for truth, and for the chance to destroy the empire that had nearly destroyed them.

Victor sneered, drawing a hidden weapon, but the betrayal of Alice and the revelation of his empire's crumbling foundation made him weak. He was no longer the manipulative, untouchable figure he once was. He was a cornered man, facing the consequences of his actions.

And in that final moment, as the tension reached its peak, Jordan made the decisive move.

Chapter 19: The Last Truth

The confrontation in the warehouse was over. The battle was won, but the war had changed them all. As the dust settled and the authorities arrived, led by an unexpected ally, the truth was revealed. The entire structure that Victor had built was now dismantled, piece by piece.

Victor was arrested, and his empire crumbled. But for Jordan, Nash, and Lila, the victory was bittersweet. They had fought for freedom, but at what cost?

As they stood on the ruins of what had once been their world, Jordan reflected on everything that had led them to this moment. Trust had been broken, but in the end, it was the bond they shared that had kept them strong.

"Did we win?" Nash asked, his voice quiet.

Jordan nodded, their gaze unwavering. "We did. But it's not about winning. It's about choosing to live on our own terms now."

Lila stood beside them, her expression soft but resolute. "And we'll make sure this doesn't happen again."

END

My name is F. N. M. Komor, but most people know me as *Sagor Sarker*. I'm from Bangladesh, a beautiful country in South Asia. Born on 01November , 1990, I have a background in Management, with both graduate and post-graduate degrees, plus an MBA in Marketing.

Writing has always been my passion, even though it's not my profession. I love reading books and exploring new ideas, and I enjoy sharing my thoughts and stories with others. Through my writing, I aim to connect with readers and bring a bit of my world to theirs.

Author: Sagor Sarker
Email: fnmkomor@gmail.com

A Smile of Betrayal

For permission requests, please contact the publisher at the email address below, addressed to "Attention: Permissions Coordinator."

Published by Self-Publishing

Author: Sagor Sarker

Email: fnmkomor@gmail.com

ISBN: 9798227166036

About the Author

My name is F. N. M. Komor, but most people know me as *Sagor Sarker*. I'm from Bangladesh, a beautiful country in South Asia. Born on 01November , 1990, I have a background in Management, with both graduate and post-graduate degrees, plus an MBA in Marketing.

Writing has always been my passion, even though it's not my profession. I love reading books and exploring new ideas, and I enjoy sharing my thoughts and stories with others. Through my writing, I aim to connect with readers and bring a bit of my world to theirs.

Read more at https://www.facebook.com/sagor.sarker.334/.